This book belongs to:

....

HarperFestival is an imprint of HarperCollins Publishers.

Based on the episode "Chores" by Jon Foster and James Lamont
Adapted by Lauren Holowaty

The Adventures of Paddington: The Wrong List

ISBN 978-0-06-298301-5

20 21 22 23 24 SCP 10 9 8 7 6 5 4 3 2 1
❖
Originally published in Great Britain by HarperCollins Children's Books in 2020
First Harper US Edition, 2020

The Adventures of Paddington™

The Wrong List

HARPER FESTIVAL

An Imprint of HarperCollinsPublishers

Dear Aunt Lucy,

Something most peculiar
happened to me today.
In fact, it seems like things
always happen to me. I'm just
that kind of bear.
I was having afternoon tea
with the Browns . . .

Mr. Brown came in carrying a tray of freshly baked scones. "Who wants jam and who wants cream?"

"Both, please!" shouted Jonathan and Judy.

"Mr. Brown," began Paddington, who was always incredibly polite, "allow me to help you . . ."

Paddington whisked the tray away from Mr. Brown, sending scones flying and the bowl of fluffy cream spinning through the air . . .

SPLaAat!

It landed smack in Mr. Brown's face!

"Oh dear. Let me get that," said Paddington, trying to lick the cream off. "We mustn't waste it."

"Ugh!" cried Mr Brown. "No, it's all right . . . I'll get a cloth from the kitchen."

"Sorry," said Paddington, thinking what else he could do. "Perhaps I could come and help you with the cleaning up?"

In the kitchen, Paddington knocked a teapot off the table by accident!

"Ahh! I really don't need any help, Paddington," Mr. Brown said, diving to catch it before it smashed. "Cleaning up is my chore."

"What's a chore?" asked Paddington.

"Everyone in the family has a chores list on the fridge," explained Mrs. Brown. "Chores are jobs, like doing the laundry or cleaning."

"How exciting! I can't wait to read my chores list!" said Paddington.

"Don't be silly, Paddington. You don't need to do family chores," laughed Mr. Brown.

The young bear looked sad. "Oh, I thought I was part of the family," he sighed, wandering off.

Mr. and Mrs. Brown hadn't meant to upset Paddington.

They called an emergency family meeting and wrote a chores list just for him. It had one thing on it—"Make Marmalade."

But when Mr. Brown went to tell Paddington that he had his very own list, it fell off the fridge!

That night, Paddington could barely sleep for excitement. A day doing chores from my very own list, he thought. It's a dream come true!

The next morning, he grabbed the first chores list he saw on the fridge. "Clean the bicycle," he read aloud. "Sounds very important."

Paddington took Mr. Brown's bicycle apart, put it in the bath, and gave it a thoroughly good clean with a toothbrush.

SCRub! SCRub! SCRub!

When the bicycle was spotless, Paddington put it back together. He couldn't remember where some bits went, but they were quite small, so he couldn't imagine they were that important.

Later, Mr. Brown came running out of the house late for work. He got on his

bicycle and . . .

BaNG! BoInG! AaRGH!
PInG! CraSH!

Next on the list was: "Polish the floorboards." Paddington thought there was rather a lot of floor. Surely that meant it needed rather a lot of polish? So he squeezed slick, oily polish all over the floor and began . . .

...sKAtIng, sLidIng,

sLippiNg,
and—
"WhoAaa!"
—falling over!

The next chore on the list simply said: "Milk." Paddington wasn't sure what that meant, so he drank all the milk.

Then he headed upstairs to do the final chore: "Wallpaper the spare room."

That sounds easier, he thought, grabbing a wallpaper brush.

As soon as the Browns came home, they stepped onto the highly polished floor and—"Whoaa!"—slid into an enormous family pileup!

"Whose chore was it to polish the floor?" asked Mrs. Bird.

Before anyone could answer, they heard a loud **CLAtter** and rushed upstairs to find . . .

. . . Paddington wallpapered to the wall! "It was the last thing on my chores list," he mumbled.

"Oh, you must've taken my list by mistake," said Mr. Brown.

Paddington explained he just wanted to be part of the family.

"You were always part of the family, Paddington," said Mrs. Brown. "You don't have to do chores to prove that."

Mr. Brown helped Paddington down when Judy gasped, "Look!" and
pointed at a drawing behind the peeling wallpaper.

"You and Jonathan drew that years ago," said Mrs. Brown. "It's a picture of the whole family."

"No it isn't," said Mr. Brown, picking up a pencil . . .

"There," Mr. Brown said, adding in a sketch of Paddington. "Now it's the whole family," he said.

The Browns thought the drawing was absolutely perfect and decided to never wallpaper the room again!

It seems there are an awful lot of chores in the world, Aunt Lucy. But being part of a family isn't one of them.

Love from
Paddington